# MINAS *and the* FISH

## Olga Pastuchiv

HOUGHTON MIFFLIN COMPANY BOSTON

1 9 9 7

For my Family and Friends

Walter Lorraine  Books

Library of Congress Cataloging-in-Publication Data

Pastuchiv, Olga.
    Minas and the Fish / by Olga Pastuchiv.
        p.      cm.
    Summary: A young boy wishes to learn to swim so he can go fishing
with his older brothers, but when a magic fish teaches him, his
brothers no longer recognize him.
    ISBN 0-395-79756-X
    [1. Fishes — Fiction.    2. Swimming — Fiction.    3. Brothers —
Fiction.]    I. Title.
PZ7.P2697Mi    1997
[E] — dc20                                                                96-24861
                                                                              CIP
                                                                              AC

For information about this and other Houghton Mifflin trade
and reference books and multimedia products, visit The Bookstore
at Houghton Mifflin on the World Wide Web at
http://www.hmco.com/trade/.

Printed in the United States of America
WOZ 10 9 8 7 6 5 4 3 2 1

Minas lived by the sea. His father and brothers were fishermen.

More than anything else, Minas wanted to go fishing with them.
But he was always told, "No, Minas, you're too little. Wait until
you get bigger and learn how to swim."

One day the brothers caught a strange fish in their nets.
"What is this?" said Antonis.
"Look at those teeth!" said Giorgos.
"And the way those eyes change colors!" said Mihalis.
They tied the fish to the mast while they hauled in their nets.

When they got home they showed the fish to everyone.
"What kind is it?" asked Giorgos.
No one had ever seen one like it before.
"Is it poisonous?" asked Antonis.
"Is it good to eat?" asked Minas.
No one knew. They went to drink their morning
coffee while they discussed their strange catch.

Minas stepped closer to get a better look.

The fish spoke, "Minas, let me go."

"What?" said Minas, looking around.

"Let me go free and I will give you a wish."

"Who's talking?" said Minas.

"I am—the fish you see before you."

"Fish don't talk," said Minas.

"Listen to me," said the fish. "A wish, anything you want."

"Can you make me big?" asked Minas.

"Yes," said the fish.

"And teach me how to swim?"

"Swim?" said the fish. "Everyone knows how to swim.
I'll make you big and I'll show you how to swim."

Minas untied the fish, and the fish made him big.

"Now jump in," said the fish. Minas jumped. The water swallowed him up. He heard the fish say, "Move your arms! Kick your legs!" Then it swam under him and held him up.

"Now do as I do," said the fish, and it swished its tail
and slid off into the water. Minas kicked and paddled.
Over and over he tried it. And then the water held him!
He felt light as a bird. He moved back and forth, fast and slow.
"Look at me!" he shouted. "I can swim!"

"Good," said the fish. "Now I will leave you.
It's time for me to go home."
"Where is your home?" asked Minas. "Can I swim there?"
"Deep in the sea. No, you can't swim there," said the fish,
"but get on my back. I will take you."

Minas saw many fish that he knew.

But as they swam deeper, the creatures

around them became more and more strange.

Some were beautiful.

Some were ugly.

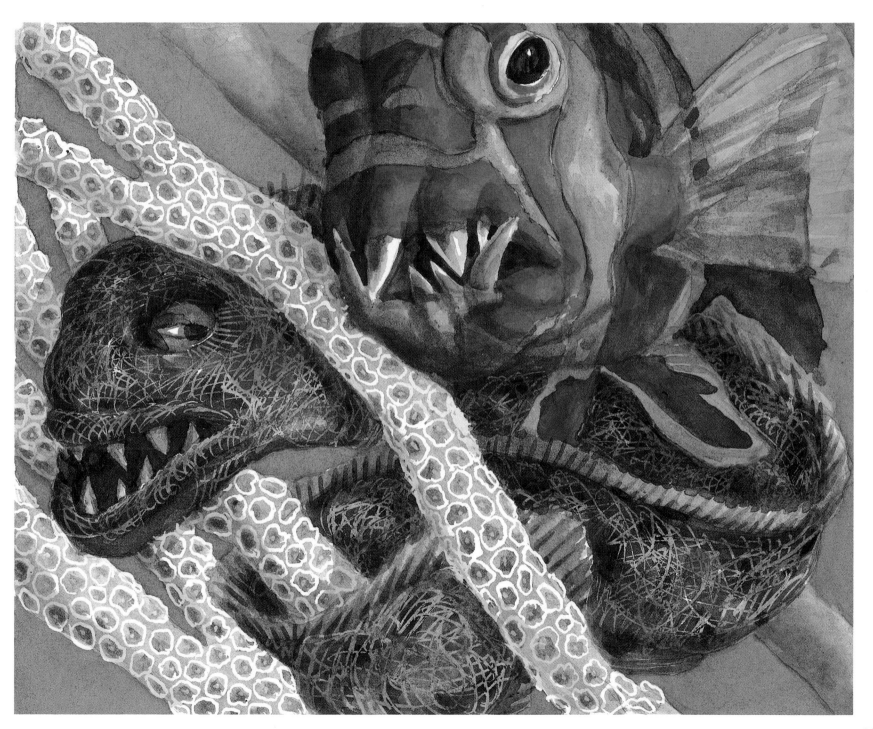

Some were very tiny.

Some were very big.

Big and scary.

Minas suddenly felt very small, and very alone.
He missed his brothers, and his mother and father.

"Fish," he whispered, "take me home now, please."

"Are you sure?" asked the fish.

"Yes, I'd like to go home now," said Minas.

So the fish took him home.

"I'm back!" shouted Minas.

His father and brothers came running.
"That's him!" they shouted. "He's the one who stole our fish!
Hey, you, where is our fish?"
"Wait!" said Minas. "Don't you recognize me?
I'm Minas. I'm big now."

"He's crazy too," said the brothers. "Where is Minas?
Did you hurt our Minas? Where's our fish? Where's Minas?"

Minas jumped back into the water to escape.
"Fish, fish!" he called. "Make me little again!
Please make me little!"

And the fish did.

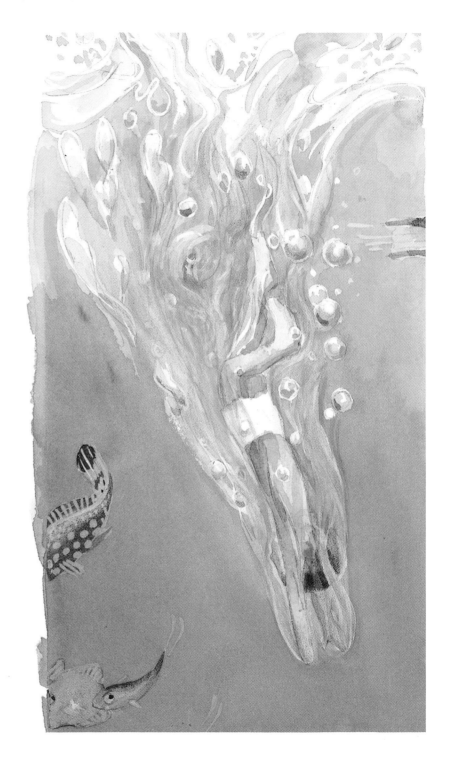

"Where did he go?" cried the brothers.
"Where's that guy who stole our fish?
Minas, what are you doing in the water?
You can't swim."
"Yes I can," said Minas. "See?"
"Look everyone, Minas knows how to swim!
You swim like a fish! But who taught you?
When? How?"

Minas said nothing.
"You're really growing up, Minas.
Come on the boat with us tonight.
You can help with the nets."

Minas was happy.